A Time Lord Christmas

A Time Lord Christmas

Matthew Petchinsky

A Time Lord Christmas: Holiday Adventures with the Doctor
By: Matthew Petchinsky

Disclaimer:
This is a fan-made work of fiction inspired by the long-running television series *Doctor Who*. It is not affiliated with, endorsed by, or connected to the BBC, its producers, writers, or official license holders. All characters, settings, and elements of the *Doctor Who* universe are the intellectual property of the BBC. This book is created for fans, as a transformative celebration of the show's legacy, blending holiday storytelling with Time Lord adventures.

Introduction

A Warm Welcome to Whovians and Festive Adventurers!

Greetings, Whovians and holiday enthusiasts alike! Whether you've just stepped out of your TARDIS or are snuggled up with a cup of hot cocoa, welcome to a unique celebration that intertwines the festive magic of Christmas with the awe-inspiring wonder of time and space. This is not just any yuletide adventure—it's a journey that transcends dimensions, bringing together the joy of the season with the boundless creativity of the Whoniverse.

For fans of *Doctor Who*, the holiday season has always carried a special significance. From epic Christmas specials to heartfelt moments that explore the triumphs and tribulations of humanity, the Doctor has a way of making the holidays both extraordinary and deeply personal. This book is an invitation to rediscover the spirit of Christmas through the lens of the Doctor's adventures—a blend of warmth, whimsy, and timeless lessons about hope, resilience, and the enduring power of kindness.

Setting the Stage for a Christmas Celebration Across Time and Space

Imagine this: snowy landscapes on alien planets, Victorian streets illuminated by gas lamps, or even the vast, glittering expanse of the universe itself—all transformed into the backdrop for Christmas adventures. With the Doctor as our guide, the season of giving and goodwill becomes an intergalactic celebration, spanning centuries and light-years.

Through this book, we'll explore the unique ways the Doctor has embraced and celebrated Christmas. From battles with terrifying alien invaders disguised as holiday decorations to quiet, reflective moments spent around crackling fires, each adventure showcases the Doctor's ability to find meaning and joy in the season—even in the face of overwhelming odds.

Christmas is a time when traditions shine brightest, but when you travel across time and space, traditions take on a whole new meaning. This book delves into how the Doctor weaves Christmas themes like family, togetherness, and hope into encounters with ancient civilizations, futuristic societies, and even parallel dimensions. The Doctor's Christmases are reminders that no matter where—or when—you are, the magic of the season can unite us all.

Explaining How the Doctor Brings Unique Holiday Cheer

What makes the Doctor's Christmas so unique? It's the way they embrace the holiday's chaos and contradictions with open arms. To the Doctor, Christmas isn't just a date on Earth's calendar; it's a feeling, a celebration of life, love, and the endless potential of the universe. Whether it's saving Earth from impending doom or offering a simple but profound gesture of kindness, the Doctor embodies the very best of what the season has to offer.

Throughout the show's storied history, the Doctor's Christmas episodes have captured everything from heart-pounding action to tear-jerking poignancy. They've reminded us that even in the darkest times, there's always a glimmer of light—a guiding star to follow. The Doctor brings a unique brand of holiday cheer by blending wisdom with child-like wonder, creating moments that are both deeply reflective and joy-fully exuberant.

So, grab your sonic screwdriver, pour yourself some eggnog, and pre-pare to journey through this festive guide. Together, we'll uncover the mysteries, marvels, and merriment of a Christmas celebrated across time and space. Because when the Doctor is involved, it's not just a holi-day—it's an adventure.

Allons-y! And Merry Christmas!

Chapter 1: The TARDIS Christmas Tree

The TARDIS has seen countless adventures, from the fiery depths of Gallifrey to the icy peaks of distant planets. But this time, the Doctor has decided it's time for a little holiday spirit within those infinite corridors. What better way to start the season than by decorating the TARDIS with a Christmas tree that's as extraordinary as the time machine itself?

Decorating the TARDIS for Christmas

The console room buzzed with its usual hum, the light from the central rotor casting a faint glow across the walls. This year, the Doctor had a festive plan: to transform the TARDIS into a holiday wonderland. A towering evergreen tree, seemingly plucked from a forest on 21st-century Earth, stood in the corner of the room. Of course, it wasn't an ordinary tree—nothing in the Doctor's world ever was.

With a snap of the Doctor's fingers, the TARDIS produced boxes of decorations from hidden compartments. Strings of lights twinkled in every imaginable color—some from Earth, others harvested from stars on distant planets. The ornaments ranged from traditional glass baubles to more peculiar items: a miniature Dalek converted into a tree topper (because "why not turn a symbol of destruction into one of joy?"), a strand of metallic garlands made from the remnants of Cybermen, and hand-carved wooden figures gifted by a village on the moon of Galleo IV.

Companions past and present had left their mark on the TARDIS tree as well. Clara's origami snowflakes hung delicately from the branches, while Amy and Rory's knitted garland wrapped around the trunk. Even River Song had contributed a dazzling blue ornament that glowed faintly—its origins, like much of River herself, shrouded in mystery.

As the Doctor added the final touches, they mused aloud, "Christmas trees are more than just decorations. They're symbols of unity—a gathering of stories, memories, and life. And what's a better symbol for the TARDIS than that?"

Exploring Alien Holiday Traditions and Ornaments

Of course, no ordinary tree would do for a time-traveling adventurer. The Doctor decided to incorporate ornaments from across the galaxy. Each decoration told a story, a snapshot of the diverse cultures the Doctor had encountered in their travels.

There were shimmering, snowflake-like crystals from the planet Yvetrex, which celebrated "Lumina," a holiday that marked the brightest day of their solar cycle. A garland of tiny glowing fungi from the forests of Xyberon symbolized their tradition of lighting the way for lost travelers. Hanging alongside these were tiny metallic spheres from Zarnath Prime, engraved with their winter constellations and filled with a fragrant mist that smelled like cinnamon and starlight.

The Doctor shared these tales while decorating, explaining the significance of each ornament. "Ah, this one's from the Haronian Ice Fields! Their 'Frost Festival' lasts for a decade, and they exchange these snow globes filled with captured auroras. And this beauty," the Doctor said, holding up a translucent orb, "is from the Baal'ni people, who believe these ornaments hold the spirit of their ancestors."

These alien traditions blended seamlessly with Earth's holiday customs, creating a tree that was not just beautiful but a testament to the unity of life across time and space.

A Mysterious Glowing Bauble That Leads to an Adventure

As the Doctor admired their handiwork, a peculiar bauble caught their eye. It was unlike any other on the tree—a small, crystalline orb that glowed faintly with an inner light. The Doctor didn't remember putting it there, nor could they recall picking it up during their travels.

Curious, the Doctor reached for the bauble, only for it to pulse brightly. A low hum filled the room, and the TARDIS seemed to react, its lights dimming momentarily. "Well, that's not good," the Doctor muttered, scanning the bauble with the sonic screwdriver.

The scan revealed something unexpected: the bauble was not an ornament at all. It was a beacon, transmitting a signal across the space-time continuum. The Doctor's face lit up with a mix of excitement and concern. "A distress call? An invitation? Or maybe both! Either way, this Christmas just got a lot more interesting."

Without warning, the TARDIS began to shake, its engines roaring to life as it locked onto the signal's origin. The console room flickered with light, and the Doctor grinned. "Hold on to your stockings! Wherever we're headed, it's bound to be an adventure."

As the TARDIS hurtled through the vortex, the mysterious bauble continued to glow, its light growing stronger as if eager to lead the way. The Doctor couldn't help but wonder what awaited them on the other side. A rescue mission? A lost civilization celebrating its own version of Christmas? Or perhaps something entirely unexpected?

Whatever it was, the Doctor knew one thing for certain: this Christmas, the TARDIS tree would be at the heart of a story that would be remembered for ages to come.

Chapter 2: A Victorian Christmas Carol

Traveling to Victorian London

The TARDIS, ever unpredictable and always dramatic, landed with its familiar wheezing groan in the heart of Victorian London. Snow fell gently over cobbled streets, and the warm glow of gas lamps illuminated a scene straight out of a Christmas card. Carolers dressed in layered cloaks and bonnets sang festive tunes, their voices carrying through the cold night air. The Doctor stepped out, adjusting their coat against the chill, a grin spreading across their face.

"Victorian London at Christmas," the Doctor said, turning to their companion (or speaking to the TARDIS if alone). "It's got all the charm, all the mystery, and a little too much soot. Perfect for a holiday adventure!"

The city bustled with the joy and chaos of the season. Horse-drawn carriages clattered along frosty streets, market stalls offered roasted chestnuts and steaming mugs of mulled wine, and children played in the snow, their laughter ringing out. But amidst the holiday cheer, the Doctor's keen eyes noticed an undertone of unease. Shadows seemed darker than usual, and an eerie chill lingered in the air—one that had nothing to do with the weather.

"Something's not quite right," the Doctor murmured, pulling out the sonic screwdriver and scanning the surroundings. The device hummed, its readings pointing toward a stately old townhouse. Above the door, an elaborate brass plaque read: **Ebenezer Scrooge, Financier and Moneylender.**

"Well, well," the Doctor said, pocketing the screwdriver. "It seems Christmas isn't the only story being told tonight. Time for a closer look!"

The Doctor Encounters a Twist on the Classic Dickens Tale

Inside Scrooge's home, the atmosphere was as gloomy as the man himself. A single candle flickered on a desk piled high with ledgers, its weak light casting long, menacing shadows. Ebenezer Scrooge, hunched over his work, muttered irritably about "wasted time" and "nonsense holidays."

The Doctor, never one for subtlety, let themselves in with a theatrical cough.

"Evening, Mr. Scrooge!" the Doctor announced, striding into the room with their characteristic energy. "I've heard a lot about you. Miserly. Grumpy. Not a fan of Christmas—though I must say, the décor could use some sprucing up. Pun absolutely intended."

Scrooge looked up, startled and annoyed. "Who are you, and how did you get in here?"

"Oh, just a passerby," the Doctor said, waving dismissively. "But I couldn't help noticing some... unusual temporal disturbances around your home. Tell me, have you noticed anything odd lately? Unexplained sounds? Flickering lights? Ghostly apparitions, perhaps?"

Scrooge's expression darkened. "If you mean the infernal spirits that have been plaguing me, then yes. But what business is it of yours?"

The Doctor leaned closer, their eyes sparkling with curiosity. "Infernal spirits, you say? Fascinating. But I don't think we're dealing with ghosts, Mr. Scrooge. Something far more sinister is at work here."

Saving Scrooge from a Malevolent Time Anomaly

As if on cue, the room grew colder, and the candle's flame flickered violently before going out entirely. The air shimmered, and three ghostly figures materialized: the Ghosts of Christmas Past, Present, and Yet to Come—or so they appeared. But the Doctor's sonic screwdriver told a different story.

"These aren't spirits," the Doctor said, scanning the figures. "They're temporal projections, fragments of a time anomaly feeding off Scrooge's emotions. Someone—or something—is manipulating the timeline."

The Ghost of Christmas Past floated forward, its translucent face twisted in malice. "Leave, Time Lord," it hissed. "This man's misery is ours to claim."

"Oh, you picked the wrong Christmas party to crash!" the Doctor retorted, stepping between Scrooge and the spectral figures. "Now, let's see who's really behind the curtain."

With a flick of the sonic screwdriver, the projections wavered, revealing their true forms: Chronovores, ancient creatures that fed on time and emotional energy. They had latched onto Scrooge's bitterness, using his pain to create a pocket of unstable time. Left unchecked, their feeding would unravel the Victorian timeline, erasing countless lives.

"Typical Chronovores," the Doctor muttered. "Always ruining holidays. Well, not on my watch!"

The battle that followed was both intellectual and physical. The Doctor, armed with the sonic screwdriver and their wit, guided Scrooge through his memories, helping him confront the moments that had hardened his heart. Each time Scrooge released a fragment of his pain—acknowledging his lost love, regretting his cruelty to Bob Cratchit—the Chronovores weakened.

Finally, the Doctor used the TARDIS to generate a temporal feedback loop, trapping the Chronovores in a fixed moment of time where they could no longer cause harm. As the creatures dissolved into nothingness, the timeline stabilized, and the oppressive chill lifted from the room.

A Changed Man and a Timeless Lesson

As dawn broke over Victorian London, Scrooge stood by his window, a changed man. The Doctor, leaning casually against the mantelpiece, watched him with a satisfied smile.

"I never thought I'd feel... hope again," Scrooge admitted, his voice tinged with wonder.

"Well, that's the thing about Christmas," the Doctor said. "It's a chance to rewrite the story, no matter how bleak it seems. And you, Ebenezer Scrooge, have all the time you need to make things right."

With a cheerful wave, the Doctor stepped back into the TARDIS. The engine's familiar sound filled the air as the time machine disappeared, leaving Scrooge to begin his new chapter.

As the TARDIS hurtled through the vortex, the Doctor couldn't help but smile. "Dickens would've loved that," they mused, flipping a switch on the console. "Now, where to next? Maybe somewhere with less Chronovores and more Christmas pudding."

And with that, the Doctor was off, ready for the next adventure—but not before making sure the spirit of Christmas was alive and well in every corner of the universe.

Chapter 3: The Ice Warriors' Frosty Feast

Visiting a Snow-Covered Mars During an Ice Warrior Holiday Celebration

The TARDIS landed softly on the surface of Mars, the usual thrum of its engines muffled by the dense frost-laden atmosphere. Outside the doors lay a pristine winter landscape. Snow blanketed the red planet's jagged terrain, turning its familiar ochre into a dazzling expanse of white. Towering ice structures shimmered in the pale sunlight, resembling crystalline cathedrals carved by nature itself. The cold was biting, even for a Time Lord.

The Doctor stepped out, clad in a heavy coat and scarf, their breath forming clouds in the frigid air. "Mars in winter," they mused. "Not something you see every day. Or every millennium, really. Perfect for a visit."

Not far from the TARDIS, the Doctor spotted the heart of Ice Warrior civilization—a sprawling network of underground tunnels and domed chambers, with a grand, frost-encrusted hall rising in the center like a glacial palace. Today was no ordinary day for the Ice Warriors. It was the eve of their most sacred holiday: **Glaciona**, a celebration of survival, unity, and the bond between their kind and the frozen elements of their world.

The Doctor marveled as they observed the Ice Warriors preparing for the feast. The typically stoic warriors displayed an unusual warmth, decorating their halls with intricate ice sculptures and glowing orbs that pulsed with a deep blue light. Massive tables were laden with Martian delicacies—gelid fruit, crystalline stalactite sweets, and frothy, steaming beverages that emitted a faint hum.

"This is remarkable," the Doctor whispered, grinning. "A people known for their strength and discipline letting their guard down for a day of joy. It's like seeing a Dalek dance—rare and wonderful!"

Unraveling a Mystery When Their Sacred Holiday Feast Is Threatened

The celebration was in full swing when a sudden, sharp sound echoed through the grand hall. The glow from the orbs flickered, and an unsettling chill descended—a stark contrast to the warmth of the festivities. The Doctor's ears perked up, sensing trouble.

The Ice Warrior chieftain, Lord Skarrlax, rose from his place at the head of the table, his voice booming. "Silence! An act of sacrilege has been committed! Our sacred feast is threatened!"

The Ice Warriors murmured among themselves, their voices a low, rumbling hiss. The Doctor, ever curious, stepped forward. "Threatened? What do you mean? Something tells me this isn't just about the roast snow-beast being overcooked."

Skarrlax eyed the Doctor with a mixture of suspicion and recognition. "Time Lord," he growled. "This is a matter of great dishonor. The keystone of our Glaciona feast—the Cryo-Heart—has been stolen."

The Cryo-Heart, the Doctor quickly learned, was an ancient artifact, said to embody the life force of Mars itself. It was the centerpiece of their celebration, a symbol of their unity and survival through the harshest of conditions. Without it, the Ice Warriors believed their feast—and their future—would be cursed.

"Sounds like something worth getting back," the Doctor said, tapping their chin. "Good thing I specialize in finding the unfindable. Now, where was it last seen?"

The Ice Warriors led the Doctor to the sacred vault where the Cryo-Heart was kept. The room was a marvel of engineering and tradition, its walls lined with glowing glyphs that told the story of the Ice Warriors' survival through millennia of ice and war. But the pedestal where the Cryo-Heart should have been was empty, a thin layer of frost marking its absence.

Using the sonic screwdriver, the Doctor scanned the area. "Ah, a residual energy trail," they murmured. "Whoever took it didn't get far. And judging by the faint traces of Zygon bioplasma... well, things just got a lot more interesting."

Diplomacy, Action, and Saving the Day

The Doctor's deduction was swift: a rogue faction of Zygons, shape-shifting aliens, had infiltrated the feast, intending to steal the Cryo-Heart to harness its immense energy. The Ice Warriors, fiercely territorial and deeply protective of their traditions, were ready to launch an all-out attack. But the Doctor knew such a conflict would devastate both species.

"No, no, no!" the Doctor exclaimed, stepping between Skarrlax and his warriors. "We're not turning this into a full-scale war. Glaciona is about unity, remember? Let's solve this with a bit of diplomacy first."

With the help of the TARDIS' sensors, the Doctor tracked the Zygons to a nearby ice cavern, where they were attempting to convert the Cryo-Heart into a weapon. The Doctor approached cautiously, armed with nothing but their wit and the sonic screwdriver.

"Hello, Zygons!" the Doctor called out cheerfully. "I understand you're trying to ruin a perfectly good holiday. Mind explaining why?"

The Zygon leader hissed, its humanoid disguise melting away to reveal its true form. "We need the Cryo-Heart's power to survive," it snarled. "Our world is gone. Mars' strength will become ours."

The Doctor nodded solemnly. "I get it. Survival is hard—believe me, I've been there. But stealing the Cryo-Heart isn't the answer. You don't have to destroy one culture to save your own. Let's find another way."

Through a mix of persuasion, empathy, and a quick display of the Cryo-Heart's unstable energy (thanks to a little sonic screwdriver tinkering), the Doctor convinced the Zygons to return the artifact. The Ice Warriors, initially furious, listened to the Doctor's plea for peace.

"Glaciona is about unity," the Doctor reminded them. "What better way to honor your traditions than by forging an alliance? Show the Zygons the strength of Mars isn't just in its ice, but in its heart."

Reluctantly, Skarrlax agreed. The Zygons returned the Cryo-Heart, and in an unprecedented act of diplomacy, the Ice Warriors invited them to share in the feast.

A Frosty Feast to Remember

With the Cryo-Heart restored, the grand hall glowed once more. The Ice Warriors and Zygons, though wary of each other, shared the meal, marking the beginning of an unlikely alliance. The Doctor watched from the sidelines, a satisfied smile on their face.

"Now this," the Doctor said, raising a steaming mug of Martian brew, "is what I call a proper holiday celebration. Peace, unity, and a bit of adventure. Just how I like it."

As the feast continued and laughter filled the air, the Doctor slipped quietly back to the TARDIS, ready for their next adventure. But for a moment, they paused to admire the snow-covered Martian landscape, the echoes of song and cheer resonating across the frozen plains.

"Merry Glaciona," the Doctor whispered, stepping inside the TARDIS. Moments later, it vanished, leaving behind only the faint sound of its engines and the lingering warmth of a holiday well spent.

Chapter 4: Christmas on Gallifrey

A Rare Glimpse of Holiday Traditions on Gallifrey

The TARDIS materialized on a rolling expanse of crimson grass under twin golden suns. The shimmering silver towers of the Citadel of the Time Lords stood in the distance, their spires piercing the vibrant, swirling orange sky. Gallifrey, home to the Time Lords, was a world often associated with order, tradition, and ancient knowledge. Yet, even this austere society had its moments of festivity.

The Doctor stepped out cautiously, scanning the horizon. "Gallifrey," they murmured, their voice tinged with nostalgia and sadness. "Home. Or at least, it was. But you'd be surprised to know that even here, we had our version of Christmas—or something close to it."

Gallifrey's holiday, known as **Celestial Convergence**, was a celebration of the turning of the Temporal Year, a time when the great celestial bodies of the Gallifreyan system aligned perfectly, creating a dazzling array of lights across the sky. It was an event steeped in symbolism: a moment to reflect on the cyclical nature of time, the resilience of life, and the infinite possibilities of the cosmos.

Time Lords, with their usual formality, marked the occasion with grand ceremonies. The Matrix Vaults were adorned with temporal glyphs, and the great halls of the Capitol echoed with solemn yet beautiful harmonies sung by the Cloister Choir. The Panopticon hosted philosophical debates on the nature of time and existence, while outside the Citadel, the simpler folk of Gallifrey—the Shobogans—lit fires in the red grasslands, exchanging stories and songs under the twin moons.

Despite the grandeur and gravity of the event, there was a warmth to it, a quiet acknowledgment that even Time Lords needed moments of connection and celebration.

Flashbacks to the Doctor's Childhood Celebrations

As the Doctor wandered through the familiar yet distant landscape, memories surfaced unbidden. They were transported to a time long before their travels, when they were just a young Time Tot, curious and full of questions.

The Doctor remembered how, as a child, they would stand with their family outside their home in the Drylands, gazing up at the night sky during Celestial Convergence. The alignment of the stars and planets created ribbons of light that danced across the heavens, illuminating the red grass with hues of gold and silver.

Their father, stern but kind, would explain the significance of the event. "Each alignment," he'd say, "is a reminder that even in chaos, there is order. And even in order, there is beauty."

The Doctor's favorite part of the celebration, however, was sneaking away to the Shobogan camps. Unlike the rigid, ceremonial traditions of the Time Lords, the Shobogans' celebrations were filled with laughter, music, and simple joys. They shared Gallifreyan spice cakes—small, dense treats that glowed faintly in the dark—and told stories of mythical beings that lived in the Time Vortex, granting wishes to the brave and foolish alike.

One particular memory stood out: a young Doctor sitting by a campfire, mesmerized by a Shobogan elder weaving a tale about the **Chrona Spirit**, a benevolent entity said to visit during the Convergence, bringing gifts of wisdom and courage to those in need. "Time is a gift," the elder had said, looking directly at the Doctor. "Use it wisely, little one."

Tying Gallifreyan Customs to Universal Holiday Themes

As the Doctor reflected on these memories, they couldn't help but draw parallels between Gallifreyan traditions and the universal themes of holidays across the cosmos.

The Doctor mused aloud, "It doesn't matter where—or when—you are. Holidays are about the same things: finding light in the darkness, sharing stories, and being reminded of what matters most. Even on Gallifrey, a world obsessed with logic and time, we celebrated hope, connection, and renewal."

The solemn debates in the Panopticon mirrored the deep conversations around Earth's hearths, where families pondered the meaning of life and love. The Shobogans' laughter and songs echoed the joy of carolers in Earth's snowy streets. And the Chrona Spirit wasn't so different from Santa Claus or other benevolent figures across the galaxy, embodying the spirit of giving and the magic of the unknown.

The Doctor found themselves standing on a hill overlooking the Citadel, their hearts heavy with the weight of what Gallifrey had become—and what it once was. Yet, in this moment, they felt a glimmer of the warmth that Celestial Convergence once brought.

Perhaps, the Doctor thought, that warmth wasn't confined to Gallifrey or any one world. Perhaps it was woven into the fabric of the universe itself, a constant amidst the chaos of existence.

With a deep breath, the Doctor turned back toward the TARDIS, a soft smile playing on their lips. "Time to share a bit of Gallifreyan holiday spirit with the rest of the universe. After all, traditions like these aren't meant to be forgotten—they're meant to be carried forward, like starlight in the dark."

And with that, the Doctor disappeared into the TARDIS, ready for the next adventure, leaving behind the crimson grasslands and the golden light of Celestial Convergence—a fleeting but eternal reminder of the beauty and resilience of life, even in the most unexpected places.

Chapter 5: The Sleigh Ride Through Space

A Malfunctioning TARDIS Lands in the Middle of an Intergalactic Sleigh Race

The TARDIS had seen its fair share of mishaps, but this one was especially dramatic. Alarms blared, sparks flew, and the rotor groaned in protest as the time machine spiraled uncontrollably through the vortex.

"Hold on, old girl!" the Doctor shouted, frantically adjusting levers and dials. "We're about to make an unscheduled stop, and I have a feeling it's going to be... festive."

With a jarring thud, the TARDIS materialized in the middle of a vast, glittering expanse of space. Outside the windows, dozens of sleighs raced through a cosmic obstacle course, their trails leaving streaks of light like comets across the star-speckled void. The TARDIS had landed squarely on the track, causing a cacophony of boos and cheers from spectators on floating platforms nearby.

"What is this?" the Doctor muttered, stepping outside and immediately ducking as a sleek, rocket-powered sleigh whizzed past, its jingle bells chiming menacingly.

A nearby official, a squat alien with antennae and a clipboard, hurried over, shouting in a garbled language. The TARDIS translated for the Doctor's benefit.

"You can't park here! You're disrupting the **Galactic Grand Sleigh Derby!**"

The Doctor raised an eyebrow. "A sleigh derby? In space? Brilliant!"

But the official wasn't impressed. "This is no ordinary race! It's a tradition as old as the universe itself. The finest pilots compete for the honor of transporting the **Celestial Gift**, a sacred artifact that symbolizes the spirit of giving. And this year, disaster has struck!"

The Doctor Must Repair the Sleigh and Win the Race to Save a Kidnapped Santa Figure

The Doctor quickly learned that the Celestial Gift had been stolen, along with the race's ceremonial figurehead—a jovial being named **Father Stellar**, who acted as a Santa-like symbol of unity across the galaxy. Without him and the artifact, the derby couldn't fulfill its purpose of spreading goodwill and joy.

The culprits? A gang of space pirates called the **Nebula Marauders**, who planned to ransom the Celestial Gift and weaponize its energy. Worse, they'd sabotaged several competitors' sleighs to ensure no one could pursue them.

"Typical pirates," the Doctor muttered. "No respect for tradition. Well, they've just earned a visit from me. But first..."

The Doctor turned to a mangled sleigh nearby, its engine sputtering weakly. Its pilot, a young alien named Klyx, looked despondent. "I was supposed to win," Klyx said. "My sleigh was my only chance to bring honor to my family. Now, it's ruined."

The Doctor knelt beside the sleigh, pulling out the sonic screwdriver. "Don't worry, Klyx. If there's one thing I'm good at, it's fixing broken things—and winning impossible races."

With a flurry of adjustments, modifications, and a little improvisation, the Doctor transformed the sleigh into a masterpiece. It was sleek, powerful, and outfitted with some unmistakable TARDIS flair—a shimmering blue exterior, glowing circuitry, and a time-loop stabilizer for extra speed.

"Now," the Doctor said, climbing into the sleigh, "let's win this race, find Father Stellar, and save Christmas for the galaxy!"

The Race Begins

The starting signal blared, and the Doctor and Klyx surged forward, the sleigh's engines roaring like a supernova. The track was a chaotic maze of asteroid fields, wormholes, and dazzling space phenomena, each more treacherous than the last.

The Doctor navigated with precision, dodging plasma bursts and weaving through collapsing star clusters. Other competitors, realizing the stakes, rallied around the Doctor, forming an impromptu alliance to outmaneuver the Nebula Marauders.

"Teamwork, everyone!" the Doctor shouted over the roar of the engines. "We're faster together!"

As the sleighs closed in on the pirates' hideout—a hulking asteroid fortress—the Doctor formulated a plan. Using the sleigh's time-loop stabilizer, they created a diversion, causing the Marauders' defenses to attack phantom sleighs instead of the real ones.

Inside the fortress, the Doctor and Klyx found Father Stellar imprisoned in a stasis field, his jolly demeanor unshaken. "Ah, the Doctor!" he exclaimed. "I had a feeling you'd show up. Care to lend a hand?"

"More like a sonic screwdriver," the Doctor quipped, disabling the stasis field. "Now, let's get you out of here."

With Father Stellar safe, the Doctor turned their attention to the Celestial Gift. The artifact pulsed with a warm, golden light, but its energy signature was unstable, a sign of the pirates' tampering.

"If this overloads, it'll take the entire system with it," the Doctor warned. "Klyx, get Father Stellar to the sleigh. I'll handle this."

Using their unparalleled knowledge of temporal mechanics, the Doctor stabilized the artifact, restoring its energy to its original, peaceful state. With seconds to spare, they raced back to the sleigh, artifact in hand.

Winning the Race and Restoring the Holiday Spirit

The Doctor and Klyx rejoined the race just in time for the final stretch. The crowd roared as the repaired sleigh streaked across the finish line, the Celestial Gift glowing brightly in the Doctor's hands.

Father Stellar, now free, delivered a rousing speech to the gathered spectators. "Thanks to the courage and ingenuity of the Doctor and Klyx, the spirit of giving is restored. Let this be a reminder that, no matter the odds, goodwill always prevails!"

As the crowd erupted in cheers, the Doctor smiled, basking in the moment. "Another Christmas saved," they said, leaning against the sleigh. "Just another day in the life of a Time Lord."

Later, as the Doctor prepared to leave, Klyx approached. "Thank you, Doctor. You've not only saved the race—you've given me hope."

The Doctor grinned, patting the young alien on the shoulder. "That's what the holidays are all about. Hope, kindness, and a bit of adventure. Now, keep racing, Klyx. The universe needs more people like you."

With a final wave, the Doctor stepped into the TARDIS, leaving behind a galaxy renewed in its celebration of unity and joy. The TARDIS dematerialized, its engines echoing like sleigh bells across the stars, a fitting end to a cosmic holiday adventure.

Chapter 6: The Dalek That Stole Christmas

A Dalek Learns the Meaning of Christmas (or Tries To)

The TARDIS materialized with a festive chime—a sound the Doctor had programmed specifically for the holiday season. The Doctor stepped out, greeted by a bustling, futuristic holiday market sprawling across the asteroid **Yuletidia**. Twinkling lights illuminated stalls selling everything from glowing ornaments to synthetic snowmakers. The air was filled with laughter, carols played on alien instruments, and the scent of spiced Martian cider.

"Ah, Christmas markets," the Doctor mused, inhaling deeply. "Even in the farthest reaches of space, everyone loves a bit of festive cheer. Unless, of course, you're a Dalek."

No sooner had the Doctor spoken than a piercing, mechanical voice shattered the joy.

"EX-TER-MI-NATE CHRISTMAS!"

The Doctor spun around to see a single Dalek rolling menacingly through the market. But this wasn't a typical extermination spree. The Dalek was snatching presents, toppling decorations, and zapping festive displays with its weapon. It screeched incomprehensibly about "inefficiency" and "irrational sentiment," sending shoppers scattering in every direction.

"Not exactly the Grinch," the Doctor muttered, "but just as destructive."

As the Dalek rolled closer, it paused, scanning the Doctor with its eyestalk. "YOU ARE THE DOC-TOR. YOU WILL EXPLAIN THIS HOLIDAY. WHY DO HUMANS ENGAGE IN SUCH ILLOGI-CAL ACTIVITIES?"

The Doctor blinked, then grinned. "You're curious? A Dalek, curious about Christmas? Oh, this is going to be fun."

A Humorous Yet Action-Packed Adventure in a Futuristic Holiday Market

The Doctor realized this Dalek was a rogue—damaged during a battle and separated from its fleet. It had stumbled upon Yuletidia, and while it understood destruction, it couldn't comprehend the bizarre sights and sounds of the market. Its directive had shifted from extermination to analysis, but its version of "analysis" involved tearing apart everything festive to understand its purpose.

The Doctor decided to use this curiosity to stall the Dalek. "All right, Dalek, let's start with the basics. Christmas is about giving. About bringing light to the darkest times of the year. You know, the complete opposite of what you do."

The Dalek whirred, processing the explanation. "GIV-ING IS IN-EFFI-CIENT. LIGHT IS IRREL-EVANT. ONLY DALEKS ARE SUPREME!"

"And yet here you are," the Doctor shot back, "alone, confused, and more obsessed with tinsel than you'd care to admit."

Their banter was interrupted by the sound of metallic clanking. A group of Daleks emerged from the far side of the market, their voices in unison: "THE ROGUE DALEK HAS COMPROMISED DALEK OPERATIONS. EXTERMINATE ALL LIFE FORMS!"

"Of course," the Doctor sighed, running toward the nearest stall. "It's never just one Dalek."

What followed was a chaotic chase through the market. The Doctor darted between stalls, flipping switches on their sonic screwdriver to turn Christmas decorations into makeshift weapons. A string of glowing lights became an electrified trap, stunning one Dalek. A snow machine, overloaded with power, created an ice slick that sent another Dalek spinning into a fountain.

Meanwhile, the rogue Dalek hesitated. It watched the festivities, its eyestalk swiveling between the chaos and the unaffected marketgoers who were still singing carols and exchanging gifts despite the invasion.

"WHY DO THEY CONTINUE?" it demanded of the Doctor. "WHY DO THEY NOT FEAR THE DALEKS?"

The Doctor, ducking behind a stall of robotic reindeer, grinned. "Because that's the spirit of Christmas. You can try to destroy it, but it always survives. Kindness, generosity, hope—they're stronger than any weapon."

The Doctor's Creative Use of Holiday Cheer to Stop a Dalek Invasion

As the other Daleks advanced, the Doctor formulated a plan. They noticed a central power hub at the heart of the market, decorated with a massive, glowing Christmas star. The star was powered by a unique energy source—pure, condensed light from a nearby neutron star.

"Perfect," the Doctor muttered, running to the hub and tinkering with the controls.

Moments later, the Doctor called out to the rogue Dalek. "Want to understand Christmas, truly understand it? Then watch this."

The Doctor activated the star, flooding the market with a radiant light that bathed everything in warmth. The light's energy disrupted the invading Daleks' systems, rendering their weapons useless and forcing them to retreat. But for the rogue Dalek, something remarkable happened. The light interacted with its damaged circuitry, triggering a cascade of memories and emotions it didn't know it had.

"EX-PERI-ENCING... UN-KNOWN DATA," the Dalek stammered. Its voice softened, almost contemplative. "THIS IS... CHRIST-MAS?"

"Yes," the Doctor said gently. "It's peace. It's love. And maybe, just maybe, it's the start of something new for you."

The rogue Dalek paused for a long moment, then turned and rolled away, disappearing into the shadows.

A New Kind of Ending

With the Daleks gone, the market erupted in cheers. The Doctor stood by the glowing star, a satisfied smile on their face.

"Another invasion stopped, another holiday saved," they said, dusting off their coat. "All in a day's work."

A child ran up to the Doctor, holding out a small, hand-carved ornament. "Here," the child said shyly. "It's for you."

The Doctor took the ornament, their hearts warmed by the gesture. "Thank you. You know, it's moments like this that make all the running worthwhile."

As the Doctor returned to the TARDIS, they glanced back at the market, now bustling with renewed energy. Somewhere out there, the rogue Dalek was beginning its own journey, its first steps toward understanding a concept far beyond extermination.

"Maybe there's hope for everyone," the Doctor murmured, hanging the ornament on the TARDIS console. With a flick of a switch, they set course for the next adventure, their hearts lighter with the knowledge that even a Dalek might one day grasp the true meaning of Christmas.

Chapter 7: The Yule Log Mystery

A Seemingly Harmless Yule Log on an Alien Planet

The TARDIS hummed softly as it landed on the planet **Firvael**, a lush, forested world blanketed in a perpetual winter glow. The air smelled of pine and frost, and the distant sound of laughter echoed through the towering crystalline trees. The Doctor stepped out into a small village nestled in a valley, its inhabitants—tall, fur-covered humanoids called the **Veynari**—gathered around a massive Yule log crackling in the center of a frozen lake.

The Yule log was a sight to behold, carved from a colossal tree and intricately adorned with glowing runes. The Veynari danced and sang around the fire, their voices resonating with a harmonic quality that seemed to merge with the forest itself. At first glance, it was a scene of perfect holiday cheer.

But as the Doctor approached, the sonic screwdriver buzzed with unusual intensity. The log emitted a strange energy signature—pulsing, alive, and far too powerful for mere wood. The Doctor frowned.

"Nothing's ever simple, is it?" they muttered.

Investigating Its Origin Uncovers an Ancient Power

The Doctor approached the village elder, a wise and stoic Veynari named **Elder Myrrak**, who greeted them warmly.

"Welcome, traveler," Myrrak said. "You have arrived at the height of our Yule celebration, a tradition that has kept our people united for centuries."

The Doctor gestured toward the glowing Yule log. "Lovely centerpiece you've got there. Mind if I ask where it came from?"

Myrrak's expression darkened. "The Yule log is sacred. It is said to carry the essence of our ancestors, binding our world together. But this year, something feels... different. The flames burn brighter, and the runes hum with an energy I cannot explain."

The Doctor nodded. "That's because it's not just a log. Whatever's powering it, it's old. Very old. And very dangerous."

Using the sonic screwdriver, the Doctor analyzed the runes and the energy emanating from the log. They discovered that the log was infused with a fragment of an **Eldritch Core**, an ancient artifact believed to predate the universe itself. The core's power had been dormant for millennia, but the Veynari's yearly rituals had inadvertently reawakened it.

The Doctor's face grew serious. "If this thing keeps building energy, it could tear a hole in the fabric of reality. Not exactly the kind of fireworks you want for a holiday celebration."

The Ancient Power Threatens the Universe

As if on cue, the Yule log flared, sending a shockwave of energy rippling through the forest. Trees cracked and splintered, and the ice beneath the villagers' feet began to fracture. The Doctor rushed to the log, shielding their eyes from the blinding light.

"It's destabilizing!" they shouted. "The core's energy is bleeding into the planet. If it's not contained, Firvael—and possibly the entire solar system—will collapse into a singularity!"

Panic spread through the village as cracks formed in the ground, releasing bursts of energy that disrupted the delicate ecosystem. Animals fled, and the crystalline trees began to wither.

"We need to shut it down," the Doctor said, turning to Elder Myrrak. "But I'll need your help."

Teaming Up with the Locals to Restore Balance

The Doctor and Myrrak quickly assembled a team of Veynari hunters and scholars, each bringing unique skills to the task. Together, they deciphered the ancient runes on the Yule log, which revealed instructions for safely neutralizing the Eldritch Core.

The Doctor explained the plan: "The core's energy must be siphoned into a stabilizing vessel. Luckily, the TARDIS can do just that. But we'll also need to restore balance to the ritual to prevent further damage to the planet."

The villagers prepared a secondary ritual, gathering elements from the forest that symbolized unity and renewal: crystalline sap from the elder trees, shimmering snow from the mountain peaks, and the bioluminescent moss that lined the lake. These components would be burned alongside the Yule log to complete the ritual and restore harmony.

As the Doctor worked to configure the TARDIS to absorb the core's energy, the Veynari faced a more immediate challenge: creatures from the planet's shadowy underlayers, drawn to the energy, began to emerge. These spectral beings, called **Voidlings**, fed on chaos and threatened to overwhelm the village.

The Doctor led the charge, rallying the Veynari to defend their home. Using torches, sonic harmonics, and ingenuity, they managed to drive back the Voidlings long enough to complete the preparations.

Restoring Balance and Saving Firvael

With the ritual ready, the Doctor and Myrrak stood before the Yule log. The Doctor connected the TARDIS to the log, initiating the energy siphon. The flames roared higher, and the ground trembled as the Eldritch Core's power flowed into the TARDIS.

"Just a little longer!" the Doctor shouted, holding the stabilizer steady.

As the last of the core's energy dissipated, the flames subsided, and the runes faded to a soft glow. The Veynari completed their ritual, their harmonic songs resonating across the forest. Slowly, the ice stabilized, the cracks healed, and the forest began to regrow.

The Doctor stepped back, breathing a sigh of relief. "And that's how you save a planet with a Yule log. Not bad for a day's work."

Elder Myrrak approached, bowing deeply. "You have our eternal gratitude, Doctor. Firvael will remember this day as the time when the spirit of Yule was truly understood."

A New Beginning

Before leaving, the Doctor joined the Veynari for a quiet moment around the now-harmless Yule log. The flames burned warmly, casting a golden light over the villagers as they shared stories and laughter.

The Doctor smiled, their hearts full. "You know, Yule isn't just about rituals or logs. It's about coming together, even when everything seems to be falling apart. And you lot? You've got that part down perfectly."

As the TARDIS dematerialized, the Doctor glanced at a small fragment of the Yule log they'd been given—a token of gratitude from the Veynari. They placed it on the console, its soft glow a reminder of yet another holiday saved through courage, unity, and just a little bit of timey-wimey brilliance.

With a flick of a switch, the Doctor set off for their next adventure, already wondering what the next chapter of their festive journey would bring.

Chapter 8: Snow Angels and Cybermen

A Chilling Adventure in a Frozen Wasteland

The TARDIS landed with an uncharacteristic shiver, its exterior coated in a thin layer of frost from the icy storm raging outside. The Doctor bundled up in a thick coat and scarf before stepping out into the unforgiving environment—a barren, frozen wasteland stretching as far as the eye could see. The air was biting, and the sky was a swirling canvas of white and gray, snowflakes tumbling like tiny frozen galaxies.

"This isn't exactly the festive atmosphere I was expecting," the Doctor muttered, scanning the area with the sonic screwdriver. The device chirped with a strange reading—one that sent a chill down the Doctor's spine, unrelated to the cold. "Energy signatures... metallic, dormant, and oh-so-familiar. That can't be good."

The wasteland, as it turned out, wasn't as barren as it seemed. Rising from the snow were jagged ice formations that glinted like crystal cathedrals. And deep within one of these formations, the Doctor spotted a glimmer of something metallic—a faint, silvery sheen embedded in the ice.

Approaching cautiously, the Doctor brushed away the frost to reveal a chilling sight: rows of Cybermen, frozen in perfect stasis, their soulless eyes staring into eternity.

Discovering Cybermen Frozen in Ice, Waiting to Be Reactivated

The Doctor's mind raced as they examined the Cybermen. These weren't just any Cybermen—they were an ancient variant, predating even the Mondasian models. Their sleek, minimalist design betrayed their age, but their weapons and systems, the Doctor guessed, were still lethal.

The sonic screwdriver buzzed urgently, indicating faint energy readings emanating from the ice. "Dormant, but not dead," the Doctor muttered. "Someone—or something—has kept them in stasis. And judging by the energy buildup, they're not planning to stay frozen for long."

As the Doctor pieced together the mystery, the ice beneath their feet cracked ominously. The ground gave way, plunging the Doctor into an underground cavern lit by an eerie blue glow. The cavern was a labyrinth of frozen corridors, and at its heart was a massive, ancient machine—pulsing with a steady rhythm, like the heartbeat of the frozen army.

The machine was a Cyber-conversion engine, modified to emit a stasis field. The Doctor realized this wasn't just a graveyard—it was a staging ground. The Cybermen had been waiting for a signal to reactivate, and the machine was on the verge of sending it.

The Doctor's Cleverness Thaws Tensions and Stops a Holiday Catastrophe

The Doctor's first instinct was to disable the machine, but as they approached, a loud, metallic voice echoed through the cavern.

"INTRUDER DETECTED. ACTIVATION SEQUENCE INITIATED."

The ice walls trembled as the Cybermen began to stir. The Doctor dashed to the machine, working furiously with the sonic screwdriver to disrupt the activation process. "Oh no, you don't!" they said, flipping switches and rerouting circuits. "No one's crashing Christmas with a Cyberman invasion—not on my watch."

Just as the first Cyberman broke free from its icy prison, the Doctor activated a holographic projector found near the machine, flooding the cavern with an unexpected sight: a hologram of children playing in the snow, building snowmen and throwing snowballs.

The Cyberman hesitated, its movements jerky and uncoordinated. The Doctor seized the moment. "You were once like them," the Doctor said, addressing the awakening Cybermen. "Living, feeling, celebrating the simple joys of life. Somewhere deep in your programming, there's still a fragment of what you used to be. You don't have to follow the directives of a machine. You can choose."

For a brief, miraculous moment, the Cybermen seemed to pause. The hologram flickered, shifting to scenes of holiday celebrations from across the galaxy—people of all species coming together in laughter and light. The cavern filled with the sound of carols, echoing off the icy walls.

But the Cyber-conversion engine continued to pulse, its signal growing stronger. The Doctor realized they needed a final solution to neutralize the threat. With a flash of inspiration, they turned the machine's energy output inward, creating a feedback loop that would permanently disable the Cybermen without destroying the cavern.

"It's not about destruction," the Doctor muttered, working quickly. "It's about balance—restoring what was lost without losing more."

As the loop completed, the Cybermen froze once more, their systems locked in stasis. The machine powered down, its blue glow fading to darkness.

A Quiet Victory in the Snow

The Doctor climbed out of the cavern as the storm above began to subside, the sky clearing to reveal a blanket of stars. They stood for a moment, gazing at the peaceful landscape, the danger averted.

"It's funny," the Doctor mused. "Even in the coldest, darkest places, there's a chance for light. You just have to know where to look."

Before returning to the TARDIS, the Doctor left a small beacon at the site—a signal to warn others of the frozen Cybermen and the dangers below. But they also left a second signal: a recording of the holograms, a message of hope and unity, in case the Cybermen ever stirred again.

As the TARDIS dematerialized, the Doctor looked back at the icy wasteland, their hearts lighter with the knowledge that even the coldest threats could be met with warmth, cleverness, and just a little bit of holiday cheer.

"Onward," they said, flipping a lever. "The universe isn't going to save itself."

Chapter 9: The Jingle Bells Paradox

A Time Loop Caused by an Enchanted Set of Jingle Bells

The TARDIS landed in a quaint little village blanketed in fresh snow, its cobblestone streets aglow with warm lamplight and bustling with last-minute Christmas Eve preparations. Carolers sang in perfect harmony, children laughed as they raced through the streets, and a small shop displayed an ornate set of jingle bells in its frosted window, shimmering faintly under the light of a nearby lantern.

The Doctor, accompanied by their companions, stepped out of the TARDIS, instantly swept up in the charm of the scene. "Christmas Eve in a village like this? You can't beat it," the Doctor said, grinning. "But those bells in the window... they're giving off an energy signature that shouldn't exist. Let's investigate, shall we?"

Inside the shop, the bells sat atop a display pedestal, radiating an otherworldly hum. The shopkeeper, a kind but harried old woman named Greta, explained their mysterious origin. "They've been in my family for generations," she said, polishing the brass bells lovingly. "No one knows where they came from, but they're said to bring good fortune to the village every Christmas."

The Doctor examined the bells with the sonic screwdriver, their expression growing more serious. "Good fortune, maybe, but these bells are temporal anomalies. They're creating a localized time disturbance. And if I'm right—"

Before the Doctor could finish, the bells emitted a piercing chime. The room shimmered, and suddenly everything went dark.

The Doctor and Companions Relive Christmas Eve

When the Doctor opened their eyes, they were back at the exact moment they'd stepped out of the TARDIS. The village was bustling as before, the carolers singing the same song, the children running past with the same laughter.

"Oh, brilliant," the Doctor groaned. "A time loop. That explains the energy readings."

Over the next few loops, the Doctor and their companions pieced together the rules of the paradox. Each cycle began with the jingle bells ringing, resetting the day to Christmas Eve morning. Despite their efforts, any attempt to remove the bells or interfere with their chime resulted in the loop resetting instantly.

"We're trapped," one companion muttered.

"No, we're not trapped," the Doctor corrected. "We're learning. Every loop is a chance to figure out what's causing this and how to stop it."

As they relived the day again and again, the Doctor began noticing subtle changes in the villagers. Some grew frustrated with the unchanging day, their cheerful façade cracking under the strain of repetition. Others became more introspective, using the loops to revisit lost opportunities or reconcile old conflicts.

For the companions, the time loop forced them to confront their own regrets and unspoken truths. One admitted a long-held grudge; another finally found the courage to express their gratitude to a loved one.

Solving the Paradox

The breakthrough came when Greta, the shopkeeper, revealed a secret: the jingle bells had once belonged to her great-great-grandmother, who was said to have been a powerful sorceress. The bells were enchanted as part of a bargain to save the village during a harsh winter centuries ago, binding time itself to ensure the village would always have a perfect Christmas Eve.

The Doctor realized the paradox stemmed from the enchantment breaking down over time. "The magic was never meant to last forever," the Doctor explained. "Time is rebelling, trying to move forward, but the bells are holding it back. The only way to fix this is to let the day end—properly."

The villagers, fearful of losing their idyllic holiday, resisted at first. "If we end the loop, what if Christmas never feels this perfect again?" one villager asked.

The Doctor knelt by a child holding a snow globe. "Christmas isn't about perfection," they said gently. "It's about the moments you share, the people you love, and the memories you create—even if they're messy. Time has to move forward, or we can't grow. We can't truly live."

With the villagers' agreement, the Doctor deactivated the bells' enchantment by combining the sonic screwdriver with a makeshift temporal stabilizer crafted from holiday decorations. As the bells chimed one final time, the village glowed with a golden light, and the time loop dissolved.

An Emotional Ending Where Everyone Learns the Value of Time

As midnight struck, the village came alive in a way it hadn't during the loops. The carolers sang with renewed joy, families embraced, and laughter echoed through the streets. The villagers, freed from the repetition of the loop, treasured every moment of the evening as if it might be their last.

Greta placed the now-silent bells back on the pedestal. "It feels... different," she said, smiling softly.

"It should," the Doctor replied. "You've given Christmas back its magic—the kind that comes from living in the present, not trying to preserve the past."

The companions, too, felt the weight of the lesson. One turned to the Doctor, their voice quiet. "We don't always appreciate how precious time is, do we?"

The Doctor smiled wistfully. "No, we don't. But that's why we have moments like this—to remind us."

As the TARDIS dematerialized, the village celebrated its first true Christmas morning in centuries. The Doctor and their companions watched from the time machine's windows, the faint sound of bells echoing in the distance.

"Onward, then," the Doctor said, flipping switches on the console. "Time waits for no one, not even us. But isn't that what makes it wonderful?"

And with that, the TARDIS disappeared into the vortex, leaving behind a village forever changed by a paradox—and the realization that time, however fleeting, is the most precious gift of all.

10: Alien Eggnog and the Invasion of the Snarfs

A Comedic Tale of an Alien Beverage Causing Mass Holiday Chaos

It all began innocently enough. At least, as innocently as things can begin when it involves alien eggnog. A mysterious vendor at a Christmas market in Cardiff introduced a strange new holiday treat—a creamy, sparkling drink labeled "Galactic Nog: A Sip of the Stars." It quickly became the season's must-have beverage, its rich, euphoric flavor leaving Earth's traditional eggnog in the dust.

Within hours, however, the festive cheer turned into sheer pandemonium. People began behaving erratically, breaking into impromptu carol-singing competitions, attempting to climb Christmas trees, and in one notable instance, using a life-sized nativity camel as a racing mount.

By the time the Doctor arrived, the city had devolved into utter chaos. The TARDIS materialized in the middle of a snow-dusted square, where two shopkeepers were locked in a slapstick battle with candy canes while a crowd cheered them on.

The Doctor stepped out, surveying the scene with bemusement. "Well, this is new. Christmas chaos isn't uncommon, but this? This has 'alien intervention' written all over it."

Scanning a discarded cup of Galactic Nog with the sonic screwdriver, the Doctor discovered the problem: the beverage contained a psychoactive compound native to the planet **Nogtril IX**. The compound caused extreme euphoria and temporary insanity in humans—and, as the Doctor suspected, had attracted some very unwelcome attention.

The Doctor Works with UNIT to Stop the Snarfs

As the Doctor was piecing together the puzzle, a familiar voice called out from behind.

"Doctor! Good timing, as usual."

It was Kate Stewart, head of UNIT, flanked by a team of operatives struggling to contain the chaos. "We've been tracking the spread of this drink for hours," Kate said, holding up a containment vial of the glowing eggnog. "We thought it was just another bizarre holiday fad until people started rioting in Santa costumes."

"And it's about to get worse," the Doctor replied grimly. "The compound in this drink isn't just an accident. It's a beacon. And if I'm right—"

A deafening roar interrupted the Doctor's thought. The sky above Cardiff shimmered, and a fleet of small, spherical ships appeared, each resembling a metallic snowball. From the ships descended the **Snarfs**, a diminutive, fur-covered alien species with oversized ears and sharp, mischievous grins.

The Doctor sighed. "Of course, it's the Snarfs. They've been trying to invade Earth for centuries. Last time, it was through counterfeit Easter eggs."

The Snarf leader, perched atop a floating podium, addressed the panicked crowd. "Attention, puny Earthlings! Your chaos has summoned us, the mighty Snarfs! We declare this planet ours—starting with your so-called 'Christmas'!"

A Battle of Wits and Eggnog

UNIT scrambled to contain the situation as the Snarfs unleashed their bizarre invasion tactics. They fired sticky tinsel cannons, deployed animated nutcracker soldiers, and unleashed weaponized snowmen that pelted citizens with exploding snowballs.

The Doctor, unfazed, darted between the chaos, formulating a plan. They quickly realized that the Snarfs weren't just exploiting the chaos—they were amplifying it. The ships in the sky emitted a frequency that enhanced the effects of the Nogtril compound, driving people into an even greater frenzy.

The Doctor turned to Kate. "We need to shut down those ships. They're the source of the signal, and without it, the Snarfs lose their advantage."

Using the TARDIS, the Doctor created a makeshift jammer that could disrupt the frequency. However, deploying it required getting past the Snarfs' defenses. With UNIT providing cover, the Doctor and a small team infiltrated one of the Snarf ships, dodging tinsel traps and animated Christmas toys.

Inside, the Doctor confronted the Snarf leader, who was gleefully orchestrating the invasion from a control panel covered in blinking lights and candy-cane levers.

"Do you really think this is going to work?" the Doctor said, leaning casually against the wall. "Earth isn't exactly known for rolling over to invaders, especially during the holidays."

The Snarf leader sneered. "Your planet is weak, distracted by meaningless traditions!"

The Doctor grinned. "Ah, but that's where you're wrong. Traditions aren't weaknesses—they're strengths. And this one?" They held up a cup of Galactic Nog. "It's about to be your undoing."

Turning the Tables

The Doctor activated the jammer, broadcasting a counter-frequency that disrupted the effects of the Nogtril compound. Almost instantly, the chaos began to subside. The Snarf ships wobbled, their systems malfunctioning as the frequency interfered with their controls.

But the Doctor wasn't finished. Using the ship's own communication system, they sent a message to the other Snarfs. "Attention, Snarf invaders! Your plan has failed. I suggest you pack up your tinsel and head home before Earth gives you a Christmas present you won't forget."

Faced with a rapidly dwindling advantage, the Snarfs retreated, their ships vanishing into the sky.

An Emotional and Festive Ending

With the Snarfs gone and the Nogtril compound neutralized, the people of Cardiff slowly returned to their senses. Despite the chaos, the village square was alive with laughter as neighbors helped each other rebuild decorations and share stories of their bizarre holiday adventure.

Kate approached the Doctor, shaking her head in disbelief. "Only you could turn an alien eggnog invasion into a victory."

The Doctor smirked, holding up a cup of regular eggnog. "It's all in a day's work, Kate. And besides, what's Christmas without a little madness?"

As the TARDIS dematerialized, the Doctor reflected on the day. "Chaos, kindness, and a planet that never stops surprising me. That's what I call a proper holiday spirit."

And somewhere, in the depths of space, the Snarfs sulked, already planning their next misguided attempt at conquering Earth—unaware that their greatest nemesis was always one step ahead, ready to defend the holidays with wit, courage, and a little festive flair.

Chapter 11: Silent Night on the Moon

A Peaceful Yet Eerie Adventure on the Moon During Christmas

The TARDIS touched down gently on the Moon's Sea of Tranquility, its familiar wheezing groan dissipating into the vast silence. The Doctor stepped out into the stillness, boots crunching softly on the fine lunar dust. Overhead, Earth glowed like a giant ornament in the black void of space, casting a faint blue light over the barren landscape.

It was Christmas Eve, but the Moon seemed far removed from the festivities taking place on Earth. Yet there was something serene about its desolation. The Doctor stood for a moment, appreciating the view.

"This is what humans always dream of, isn't it?" the Doctor mused aloud. "Peace, quiet, and a view that makes you feel small in the best possible way."

But the tranquility was soon interrupted. On the horizon, faint figures appeared, shimmering against the backdrop of stars. They moved slowly, their forms indistinct, but the sound that accompanied them was unmistakable—haunting, ethereal voices singing a soft rendition of "Silent Night."

The Doctor frowned. "Carollers? On the Moon? That's... unusual."

Encountering the Mysterious "Lunar Carollers" with a Dark Secret

The Doctor approached cautiously, their curiosity piqued. The figures became clearer as they drew near: humanoid shapes cloaked in flowing, silvery robes that seemed to ripple like liquid under the light of Earth. Their faces were obscured, hidden beneath hoods that glowed faintly.

The Doctor raised a hand in greeting. "Hello there! Lovely singing. Didn't think the Moon had a choir."

The figures stopped, their song fading into silence. One stepped forward, its voice low and melodic. "We are the **Lunar Carollers**, guardians of the silent night. Who are you to disturb our vigil?"

"I'm the Doctor," they replied, holding up the sonic screwdriver. "And I'm just passing through, though I must say, you've got quite the setup here. Guardians of the silent night, you say? Sounds important."

The figure tilted its head. "The Moon is a place of stillness, a sanctuary. We ensure it remains so, especially on this sacred night."

But something felt off. The Doctor noticed faint distortions around the figures, as if their forms weren't entirely real. The sonic screwdriver buzzed faintly in warning, detecting an energy field that seemed to warp space-time.

"You're not just singers, are you?" the Doctor said, narrowing their eyes. "There's something else going on here."

The Dark Secret of the Lunar Carollers

As the Doctor investigated further, the truth about the Lunar Carollers began to unravel. They weren't guardians or benevolent spirits—they were manifestations of an ancient alien intelligence known as the **Nocturnis Field**, a sentient energy form that had long slumbered beneath the Moon's surface.

The Nocturnis Field had awakened during a lunar excavation decades earlier, feeding off the memories and emotions of humans who had visited the Moon. Over time, it had developed a fascination with Earth's traditions, particularly Christmas. The carollers were its attempt to mimic human celebration, but the Nocturnis Field didn't understand the concept of joy—it only knew how to replicate emotions it had absorbed, and in doing so, it created an unsettling parody of human customs.

Worse, the Nocturnis Field's energy was growing unstable. Its attempts to sustain the carollers were causing ripples in the Moon's gravitational field, threatening to destabilize Earth's tides.

The Doctor stood in the center of the carollers, addressing the Nocturnis Field directly. "You're not evil. You're just... lonely, aren't you? Trapped here, watching Earth, yearning to connect but not knowing how."

The carollers paused, their forms flickering. A deep, resonant voice echoed across the lunar surface. "Lonely... yes. Alone... for centuries. Observing... never part of it."

The Doctor nodded. "But this isn't the way. You're hurting the very world you admire. If you want to understand humans, you have to let them be. Let their traditions remain their own."

The Doctor Solves the Mystery and Restores Peace

The Nocturnis Field was reluctant to release its hold. The Doctor worked quickly, using the sonic screwdriver and the TARDIS' systems to stabilize the energy field. They reconfigured the Field's energy, creating a harmonic resonance that allowed it to project itself into Earth's radio waves without disrupting the Moon's stability.

"There," the Doctor said, wiping their hands. "Now you can observe and listen as much as you like. Humanity's music, their stories—they'll all be there for you, but from a safe distance."

The carollers dissolved, their forms fading into shimmering particles that drifted upward like snowflakes. The Nocturnis Field's voice echoed one last time. "Thank you... Doctor. We will... listen."

As the Moon returned to its natural stillness, the Doctor sat on a rock, gazing up at Earth. "A sentient energy field trying to understand Christmas," they said, chuckling softly. "It's always something."

A Moment of Reflection

Before leaving, the Doctor set up a small transmitter on the lunar surface, broadcasting Earth's Christmas carols into the void for the Nocturnis Field to enjoy. It was a simple gesture, but one that carried profound meaning—a reminder that even in the vast emptiness of space, connections could be forged.

Back in the TARDIS, the Doctor looked once more at the blue and white jewel of Earth. "Silent nights are rare," they said softly. "But when you find one, it's worth cherishing."

With that, the TARDIS dematerialized, leaving the Moon bathed in the gentle light of Earth, its silence restored and its mysterious carollers now part of a larger, ongoing story of understanding and connection.

Chapter 12: The First Noel Across Time

Traveling Back to the First Christmas

The TARDIS hummed with excitement as the Doctor entered coordinates that few Time Lords had dared to explore: ancient Judea, on a night that would resonate across millennia. The Doctor, accompanied by their companions, had decided to witness a pivotal moment in history—the first Christmas, a night steeped in myth, tradition, and cultural significance.

As the TARDIS materialized quietly on a hillside overlooking Bethlehem, the Doctor adjusted their scarf, glanced at the glowing skyline, and smiled. "There it is," they said softly, gesturing toward the small town bathed in moonlight. "Bethlehem, under the Roman Empire. A humble night that would spark traditions celebrated across galaxies. And we're right in the heart of it."

The companions stepped out, marveling at the simplicity of the scene. Shepherds tended their flocks under the stars, while a distant melody of a flute carried on the wind. Above them, a bright star shone unnaturally bright—a cosmic beacon that guided travelers toward the stable where a child was said to have been born.

But the Doctor's eyes narrowed as the sonic screwdriver emitted a faint warning beep. Something wasn't right. The star wasn't just bright—it was pulsating with temporal energy.

"Of course," the Doctor muttered. "Someone's tampering with history. We're not here alone."

Protecting History from Time-Traveling Villains

The Doctor traced the temporal disturbance to a group of time-traveling villains called the **Chronomancers**, rogue scientists from a distant future who sought to manipulate pivotal moments in history for their own gain.

Hidden in the shadows near the stable, the Doctor spotted the Chronomancers' advanced equipment—energy relays disguised as Roman tools, aimed at redirecting the star's light to create a temporal rift. Their goal was to erase the significance of the night, thereby disrupting centuries of human traditions tied to the story.

The Doctor's companions whispered anxiously. "Why would they want to disrupt this moment? Isn't it just a simple birth?"

The Doctor turned, their expression serious. "It's never just about the moment. It's about the ripple effect. Christmas isn't just a day—it's an idea, a symbol of hope and kindness that's endured for thousands of years. Without it, countless acts of goodwill and compassion might never happen. The Chronomancers know that. They're trying to unwrite humanity's potential for light in the dark."

Steeling themselves, the Doctor approached the Chronomancers' leader, a cold, calculating figure named **Vorian**, who smirked at their arrival.

"Doctor," Vorian said, mockingly. "Always meddling in things you don't understand. We're not erasing history—we're perfecting it."

"Perfecting it?" the Doctor shot back. "By erasing its heart? History isn't meant to be perfect, Vorian. It's messy, unpredictable, and full of contradictions. But that's what makes it beautiful. And you're not rewriting it on my watch."

A Battle of Wits and Courage

The confrontation escalated as the Doctor and their companions worked to dismantle the Chronomancers' devices. Using their sonic screwdriver, the Doctor disabled several energy relays, but the Chronomancers countered by deploying temporal drones—small, glowing orbs that buzzed menacingly as they worked to repair the damage.

"Keep them busy!" the Doctor shouted, directing their companions to distract the drones while they scrambled to sever the main relay connecting the star to the rift.

The battle was both physical and intellectual, with the Doctor outsmarting the Chronomancers at every turn. They used the environment to their advantage, tricking the drones into herding sheep that blocked the Chronomancers' equipment, while redirecting the energy pulses into harmless bursts of light.

At one point, Vorian cornered the Doctor, brandishing a temporal disruptor. "You can't stop us, Doctor. The universe doesn't need hope—it needs order."

The Doctor smiled grimly. "The universe doesn't need your kind of order, Vorian. It thrives on hope. And that's one thing you'll never be able to erase."

With a final, calculated move, the Doctor reversed the star's energy flow, sending a brilliant cascade of light across the night sky. The rift closed, and the Chronomancers, unable to counter the energy surge, retreated into the vortex with a hiss of frustration.

A Heartwarming Finale

As the dust settled, the Doctor and their companions stood on the hill, watching as the star resumed its natural glow. Below them, the stable was quiet and still, illuminated by the gentle light of the heavens.

"Did we really just save Christmas?" one companion asked, still catching their breath.

The Doctor chuckled. "Not Christmas itself. Just its chance to shine. Humanity will do the rest. This night—it's not just about a single story. It's about what it inspires in people, generation after generation."

The companions fell silent, watching as the shepherds made their way toward the stable, guided by the light. In that moment, the simplicity and grandeur of the scene hit them all.

The Doctor, uncharacteristically quiet, gazed up at the star. "Time is funny," they said softly. "Moments like this—they ripple outward, touching lives in ways we'll never fully understand. And that's the beauty of it. The story isn't just theirs anymore. It belongs to everyone who hears it, who passes it on, who finds meaning in it."

As the TARDIS prepared to dematerialize, the Doctor left a small gift—a glowing orb that would emit soft, harmonic music to blend with the night's quiet song. A gesture, they hoped, that would echo through the ages as a subtle, added note to the story.

Inside the TARDIS, the companions reflected on what they'd witnessed. "So, this is the true spirit of the season?" one asked.

The Doctor smiled warmly. "It's hope, generosity, and the simple act of being there for one another. Whether it's on a quiet hill in Judea or halfway across the stars, that's what really matters."

As the TARDIS disappeared into the vortex, the light of the star shone on, a symbol of resilience, compassion, and the unending power of belief. And for a fleeting moment, even the Doctor felt a small, rare sense of peace.

Appendix

Behind-the-Scenes Look at the Doctor's Holiday-Themed Gadgets

Over the centuries, the Doctor has encountered countless holiday challenges, from alien invasions to temporal anomalies, and always finds inventive ways to solve them. Here's a closer look at some of the Doctor's most festive gadgets:

1. The Sonic Screwdriver (Holiday Edition)

While the standard sonic screwdriver is already versatile, the Doctor often tweaks it for holiday adventures.

- **Festive Frequency Mode:** Emits a harmonic soundwave that can synchronize with holiday songs, disorienting enemies or enhancing the mood.
- **Tinsel Launcher Attachment:** Shoots festive tinsel at high velocity—great for both decorating and immobilizing foes.
- **Bauble Scanner Function:** Scans and detects energy signatures within seemingly harmless holiday ornaments, useful for uncovering alien tech disguised as decorations.

2. The Christmas Circuit Stabilizer

Built from salvaged parts of Cybermen technology and holiday lights, this device can stabilize time loops caused by temporal anomalies during the holidays.

- **Appearance:** A glowing star-shaped gadget that can be hung like an ornament.
- **Key Feature:** Emits a "time-freezing" field to slow chaotic events during critical moments.

3. The Eggnog Analyzer

Introduced in *The Dalek That Stole Christmas,* this gadget detects harmful or alien compounds in holiday drinks.

- **Secondary Feature:** Can also heat beverages to the perfect temperature for sipping.

4. Holo-Wreath Projector

A portable device that projects three-dimensional holographic wreaths.

- **Uses:** Great for creating instant holiday ambiance or distracting enemies with bright, spinning decorations.
- **Bonus:** Can be programmed to emit soothing seasonal scents like pine, cinnamon, or roasted chestnuts.

5. Temporal Ornament Beacon

Crafted by the Doctor to ensure Earth's traditions remain safe from tampering.

- **Design:** Resembles a snow globe with swirling time particles inside.
- **Purpose:** Emits a signal that stabilizes local history, ensuring key moments remain intact.

Holiday Recipes from Across the Universe

The Doctor has dined on delicacies from countless worlds, and these are some of the most festive recipes they've encountered:

1. Glorban Spice Cakes (Planet Glorban)

A dense, glowing cake enjoyed by the Shobogans during the Doctor's childhood on Gallifrey.

- **Ingredients:**
    - 2 cups of flour (substitute with neutron-dust flour for authenticity—Earth flour works fine!)
    - 1 teaspoon of starfruit zest (or lemon zest)
    - ½ teaspoon cinnamon
    - ½ teaspoon nutmeg
    - 1 cup honey
    - ¼ cup of glowing sugar crystals (optional; substitute with colored sugar).
- **Instructions:**
    - Mix dry ingredients, then slowly fold in honey.
    - Bake at 180°C (350°F) for 25 minutes.
    - Sprinkle glowing sugar crystals on top before serving.

2. Xyberon Frostberry Punch

A warm, fizzy drink from the frost-covered planet Xyberon.

- **Ingredients:**
  - 2 cups frostberry juice (substitute with cranberry juice)
  - 1 cup sparkling water
  - 2 tablespoons of Martian spice nectar (or honey)
  - 1 cinnamon stick
- **Instructions:**
  - Heat frostberry juice and cinnamon stick over low heat.
  - Add honey and stir until dissolved.
  - Pour into cups and top with sparkling water for a fizzy finish.

3. Jaxaphorian Star Pies

Small, star-shaped pastries popular during celestial festivals.

- **Ingredients:**
  - 1 sheet puff pastry
  - 1 cup mixed fruit preserves (your choice of flavors)
  - 1 egg (for egg wash)
  - Powdered sugar (for dusting)
- **Instructions:**
  - Cut puff pastry into star shapes.
  - Place a small spoonful of fruit preserves in the center of half the stars.
  - Cover with another star and seal the edges with a fork.
  - Brush with egg wash and bake at 200°C (400°F) for 15 minutes.
  - Dust with powdered sugar before serving.

A Guide to Creating Your Own TARDIS-Inspired Christmas Decorations

Bring a touch of timey-wimey charm to your holiday décor with these TARDIS-inspired projects!

1. TARDIS Ornament

- **Materials Needed:**
    - Small blue cardboard or plastic box (or paint a mini wooden crate blue).
    - White paint or marker for windows.
    - Black marker for the "POLICE PUBLIC CALL BOX" sign.
    - Silver string or ribbon to hang.
- **Instructions:**
    - Paint or decorate your box to resemble the TARDIS.
    - Add details like windows, signs, and even a small light at the top.
    - Attach a ribbon or string to hang it on your tree.

2. TARDIS Wreath

- **Materials Needed:**
    - A standard wreath (real or artificial).
    - Blue lights or garlands.
    - Small TARDIS figurines or ornaments.
    - Silver tinsel for a time vortex effect.
- **Instructions:**
    - Wrap the wreath in blue lights and garlands.
    - Attach TARDIS figurines or ornaments with wire or string.
    - Add silver tinsel for a swirling, festive effect.

3. Time Vortex Garland

- **Materials Needed:**
    - Black ribbon or string lights.
    - Clear plastic ornaments.
    - Glow-in-the-dark paint.
    - Glitter (optional).
- **Instructions:**
    - Paint swirling patterns on the ornaments with glow-in-the-dark paint.
    - Fill the ornaments with glitter for extra sparkle.
    - String them along the black ribbon or lights for a garland reminiscent of the time vortex.

4. Sonic Screwdriver Stocking Hanger

- **Materials Needed:**
    - A toy or replica sonic screwdriver.
    - Strong adhesive or hook.
    - Holiday ribbon.
- **Instructions:**
    - Attach the sonic screwdriver to the mantle with adhesive or a hook.
    - Wrap holiday ribbon around the base for a festive touch.
    - Use it to hang stockings with a time-traveling flair.

With these gadgets, recipes, and decorations, you'll be ready to celebrate the holidays in true Doctor Who style. Whether you're baking intergalactic treats or hanging TARDIS ornaments, remember that the spirit of the season is all about connection, creativity, and a dash of adventure!

<u>Message from the Author:</u>

I hope you enjoyed this book, I love astrology and knew there was not a book such as this out on the shelf. I love metaphysical items as well. Please check out my other books:

-Life of Government Benefits

-My life of Hell

-My life with Hydrocephalus

-Red Sky

-World Domination:Woman's rule

-World Domination:Woman's Rule 2: The War

-Life and Banishment of Apophis: book 1

-The Kidney Friendly Diet

-The Ultimate Hemp Cookbook

-Creating a Dispensary(legally)

-Cleanliness throughout life: the importance of showering from childhood to adulthood.

-Strong Roots: The Risks of Overcoddling children

-Hemp Horoscopes: Cosmic Insights and Earthly Healing

- Celestial Hemp Navigating the Zodiac: Through the Green Cosmos

-Astrological Hemp: Aligning The Stars with Earth's Ancient Herb

-The Astrological Guide to Hemp: Stars, Signs, and Sacred Leaves

-Green Growth: Innovative Marketing Strategies for your Hemp Products and Dispensary

-Cosmic Cannabis

-Astrological Munchies

-Henry The Hemp

-Zodiacal Roots: The Astrological Soul Of Hemp

- Green Constellations: Intersection of Hemp and Zodiac

-Hemp in The Houses: An astrological Adventure Through The Cannabis Galaxy

-Galactic Ganja Guide

Heavenly Hemp

Zodiac Leaves

Doctor Who Astrology

Cannastrology

Stellar Satvias and Cosmic Indicas

Celestial Cannabis: A Zodiac Journey

AstroHerbology: The Sky and The Soil: Volume 1

AstroHerbology:Celestial Cannabis:Volume 2

Cosmic Cannabis Cultivation

The Starry Guide to Herbal Harmony: Volume 1

The Starry Guide to Herbal Harmony: Cannabis Universe: Volume 2

Yugioh Astrology: Astrological Guide to Deck, Duels and more

Nightmare Mansion: Echoes of The Abyss

Nightmare Mansion 2: Legacy of Shadows

Nightmare Mansion 3: Shadows of the Forgotten

Nightmare Mansion 4: Echoes of the Damned

The Life and Banishment of Apophis: Book 2

Nightmare Mansion: Halls of Despair

Healing with Herb: Cannabis and Hydrocephalus

Planetary Pot: Aligning with Astrological Herbs: Volume 1

Fast Track to Freedom: 30 Days to Financial Independence Using AI, Assets, and Agile Hustles

Cosmic Hemp Pathways

How to Become Financially Free in 30 Days: 10,000 Paths to Prosperity

Zodiacal Herbage: Astrological Insights: Volume 1

Nightmare Mansion: Whispers in the Walls

The Daleks Invade Atlantis

Henry the hemp and Hydrocephalus

10X The Kidney Friendly Diet

Cannabis Universe: Adult coloring book

Hemp Astrology: The Healing Power of the Stars

Zodiacal Herbage: Astrological Insights: Cannabis Universe: Volume 2

<u>Planetary Pot: Aligning with Astrological Herbs: Cannabis Universes: Volume 2</u>

Doctor Who Meets the Replicators and SG-1: The Ultimate Battle for Survival

Nightmare Mansion: Curse of the Blood Moon

<u>The Celestial Stoner: A Guide to the Zodiac</u>

Cosmic Pleasures: Sex Toy Astrology for Every Sign

Hydrocephalus Astrology: Navigating the Stars and Healing Waters

Lapis and the Mischievous Chocolate Bar

Celestial Positions: Sexual Astrology for Every Sign

Apophis's Shadow Work Journal: : A Journey of Self-Discovery and Healing

Kinky Cosmos: Sexual Kink Astrology for Every Sign

Digital Cosmos: The Astrological Digimon Compendium

Stellar Seeds: The Cosmic Guide to Growing with Astrology

Apophis's Daily Gratitude Journal

Cat Astrology: Feline Mysteries of the Cosmos

The Cosmic Kama Sutra: An Astrological Guide to Sexual Positions

Unleash Your Potential: A Guided Journal Powered by AI Insights

Whispers of the Enchanted Grove

Cosmic Pleasures: An Astrological Guide to Sexual Kinks

369, 12 Manifestation Journal

Whisper of the nocturne journal(blank journal for writing or drawing)

The Boogey Book

Locked In Reflection: A Chastity Journey Through Locktober

Generating Wealth Quickly:

How to Generate $100,000 in 24 Hours

Star Magic: Harness the Power of the Universe

The Flatulence Chronicles: A Fart Journal for Self-Discovery

The Doctor and The Death Moth

Seize the Day: A Personal Seizure Tracking Journal

The Ultimate Boogeyman Safari: A Journey into the Boogie World and Beyond

Whispers of Samhain: 1,000 Spells of Love, Luck, and Lunar Magic: Samhain Spell Book

Apophis's guides:

Witch's Spellbook Crafting Guide for Halloween

<u>Frost & Flame: The Enchanted Yule Grimoire of 1000 Winter Spells</u>

<u>The Ultimate Boogey Goo Guide & Spooky Activities for Halloween Fun</u>

Harmony of the Scales: A Libra's Spellcraft for Balance and Beauty

The Enchanted Advent: 36 Days of Christmas Wonders

Nightmare Mansion: The Labyrinth of Screams

Harvest of Enchantment: 1,000 Spells of Gratitude, Love, and Fortune for Thanksgiving

The Boogey Chronicles: A Journal of Nightly Encounters and Shadowy Secrets

The 12 Days of Financial Freedom: A Step-by-Step Christmas Countdown to Transform Your Finances

Sigil of the Eternal Spiral Blank Journal

A Christmas Feast: Timeless Recipes for Every Meal

If you want solar for your home go here: https://www.harborso-lar.live/apophisenterprises/

Get Some Tarot cards: https://www.makeplayingcards.com/sell/apophis-occult-shop

<u>**Get some shirts: https://www.bonfire.com/store/apophis-shirt-emporium/**</u>

<u>Instagrams:</u>
@apophis_enterprises,
@apophisbookemporium,
@apophisscardshop
Twitter: @apophisenterpr1
 Tiktok:@apophisenterprise
Youtube: @sg1fan23477, @FiresideRetreatKingdom
Hive: @sg1fan23477
CheeLee: @SG1fan23477

Podcast: Apophis Chat Zone: https://open.spotify.com/show/5zXbrCLEV2xzCp8ybrfHsk?si=fb4d4fdbdce44dec

 –

Newsletter: https://apophiss-newsletter-27c897.beehiiv.com/

www.ingramcontent.com/pod-product-compliance
Lightning Source LLC
Chambersburg PA
CBHW072112150726
47999CB00005B/2009